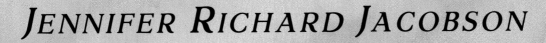

JENNIFER RICHARD JACOBSON

A Net of Stars

PICTURES BY GREG SHED

**Dial Books
for Young Readers**
New York

For Holly, who is brave

—J. R. J.

For Simi, Katie, and Alex

—G. S.

Published by Dial Books for Young Readers
A member of Penguin Putnam Inc.
375 Hudson Street
New York, New York 10014

Text copyright © 1998 by Jennifer Richard Jacobson
Pictures copyright © 1998 by Greg Shed
Designed by Nancy R. Leo
Printed in Hong Kong
First Edition
1 3 5 7 9 10 8 6 4 2

Library of Congress Cataloging in Publication Data
Jacobson, Jennifer Richard, date.
A net of stars/ by Jennifer Richard Jacobson; pictures by Greg Shed.—1st ed.
p.   cm.
Summary: When the carnival comes to town, Etta finds an ingenious way
to overcome her fear of heights.
ISBN 0-8037-2087-4.—ISBN 0-8037-2088-2 (lib.)
[1. Fear—Fiction. 2. Ferris wheels—Fiction.] I. Shed, Greg, ill. II. Title.
PZ7.J1529Ne 1998   [E]—dc20   96-33819   CIP   AC

The art was rendered in gouache on canvas.

At haying time the midway comes to town.

Harper and Fiona and I finish all our lima beans quick so we can stand by the fence and watch the rides go up.

"There's the zipper!" shouts Fiona.

You have to be eight to ride the zipper. Only Fiona and Harper are allowed. I look up. "This year," I say, "I'm going to ride the Ferris wheel."

"You say that every year," says Harper. "But you'll chicken out. You always do."

I won't, I think. *This year I'll be brave.*

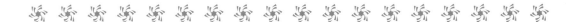

The next morning I can see the top of the Ferris wheel from our front porch. I wonder what it's like to be so high. I decide to practice.

I drag the ladder from the shed to the chicken coop. I climb
the rungs until I come to the next to last one. Then I crawl like
a big old daddy longlegs up the tar-paper roof. I don't mind
the highness 'til I reach the tippy-top.

I sit down quick and look up at the blue sky above me. It seems so deep and so empty and I remember Fiona saying that the whole world turns. What if it turns now and I fall into the sky? What would catch me?

"What are you doing?" yells Harper. I don't say anything.
I'm afraid if I talk, my own breath will carry me off this roof.
Harper gets Fiona, and Fiona holds me so I can get down.

"Not everyone likes high places, Etta-berry," says Fiona.
But it doesn't make me feel better.

The midway opens right after lunch.

"Stay with Fiona!" Mama calls as we race away with clean shirts and a whole ten-dollar bill. Fiona tries to hold my hand. I pretend I don't see.

Everything is noisy and colorful and whirling at the midway. We ride a yellow teacup that spins me so fast—I laugh but I can't hear my sound. I go in a crazy house and roll in a barrel. Fiona and Harper go on the zipper, and I ride a white horse named Pearly Princess.

"I want to ride the Ferris wheel now," I say.

"Are you sure?" asks Fiona.

"She won't do it," says Harper.

We give our tickets to a man with a tattoo who snaps a bar across my lap, and I now let Fiona take my hand. I have never been this far.

"Stop rocking the car, Harper," says Fiona, but I don't mind the back and forth. The wheel turns and our rocking seat lifts higher and higher into the air. When I look up, all I see is deep sky. I feel like I'll fall and fall and fall. *Be brave,* I say. *Can't be brave. Can't!* I hold on to Fiona as hard as I can and I start to cry. Big tears I cry. Big baby tears.

The man with the tattoo stops our seat, then lets me out. I stand on dusty ground and watch Fiona and Harper go around and around and around. They wave to me, but I don't wave back.

I don't feel like talking 'til after dinnertime. Mama gives us Popsicles and tells us to eat them on the front porch.

"There's the Big Dipper," says Harper.

"It's the mama bear," says Fiona.

"Who's the mama bear?" I ask.

"People used to imagine lines between the stars to make pictures," says Fiona. "Follow my finger and I'll show you the bear."

I make my finger go where Fiona says, but I don't see the bear.

That night I get up and look out my window. I look so hard, my squinty eyes make the stars sparkle closer together. Then I see them! I see a baby bear, and a mama bear too! I stay up a long time looking at pictures in the sky.

And then I know.

At breakfast Fiona and Harper ask if they can go back to the midway. "If you use your chore money," says Mama. "It's up to you."

"I don't want to go," I say.

"I have money, Etta," says Fiona. "I'll buy you some tickets for the rides."

"No thanks," I say. "I'm waiting."

"Waiting for what?" asks Harper.

"For dark," I say.

Harper gives me a funny look. "Suit yourself," he says.

Waiting's hard. I keep looking up to see where the sun is.
Fiona and Harper come back talking about the zipper. I don't
want to listen to their words. I wish nighttime would come.
Finally Daddy dries the last dinner dish. "Let's go," he says.

We always go back to the midway on the last night when
Daddy plays bingo. Now the midway looks like a fairyland
with rainbow lights. The carnival music sounds louder than
the roller coaster screams.

✻ ✻ ✻ ✻ ✻ ✻ ✻ ✻ ✻ ✻ ✻ ✻ ✻ ✻ ✻ ✻

"Stay together," says Daddy, and he disappears into the smoky bingo tent. Fiona and Harper pay fifty cents to try and win a prize.

I don't say anything. I run over to the woman in the booth and buy the right number of tickets. The tattoo man takes my tickets and snaps the bar across my lap. I close my eyes tight tight, and feel the chair go up. I know I'm getting higher. I know I'm in the sky. When I'm sure I'm at the top, I open my eyes and look up.

✻ ✻ ✻ ✻ ✻ ✻ ✻ ✻ ✻ ✻ ✻ ✻ ✻ ✻ ✻ ✻

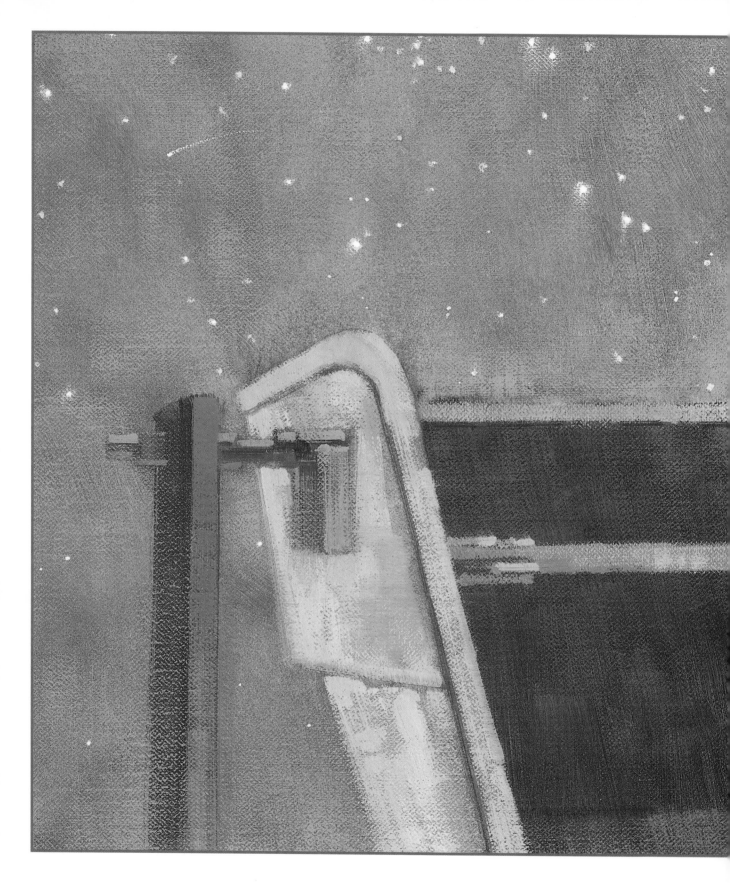

I see stars. Stars so close I can touch them. I draw a line from
star to star to star. *There,* I think. I have a net. If the whole world

should turn, and I fall into the sky, a net of stars will catch me.
The big yellow moon smiles. I AM BRAVE.

"Etta!"
I look down and see Harper searching for me.
"Up here!" I yell as loud as I can.
Harper looks up and sees me. He shows Fiona where I am.
Fiona and Harper watch me go around and around. They wave.

This time I wave back.